Kahan Tum Chale Gaye!

Flairs and Glairs

Publication House

"Kahan Tum Chale Gae!"

ISBN No: " 978-93-90799-98-5"

1st Edition

Language – English and Hindi

Flairs and Glairs

Publication House

Regd. Under MSME Act.

Disclaimer

This is a work of fiction and solely represent the thoughts of the corresponding authors of the articles. Our editors have tried their best to edit the content of all the authors and check the plagiarism.

All the write-ups in this book are unique and are only published in this book.

In case any plagiarism or error is found, only the author is responsible alone, and not the publisher or the Compilers.

Cover Designing and Book Formatting

Shubham Shah and Ishani Agarwal

Acknowledgement

First of all, I thank God, for this life, as a human, has been a lesson full of experiences that have moulded me into the person I am today. To destiny, for teaching me lessons that no one else could.

I'd like to thank my parents for their support, without them, I'd be nothing. My sibling, my love, and my co-compiler, Nishita Ninave, for her help, support and the blessing she is in my life.

I pay gratitude to my friends Avnish Kumar, Alolika Ray, Momo, Pavan Sharma, Ankita Kumar, and Anandhini Iyappan. You people are not just my friends but are my guiding angels who I know I can blindly rely upon.

Shubham Shah and the entire team of Flairs and Glairs, I salute your dedication and helping nature. You are the reason why the book was possible.

Last but not the least, all the co-authors who were extremely cooperative throughout the project. You all are the whole and soul of the book. All I wish is health and happiness for you all!

Grishma Ninave

Firstly I would like to thank God for the blessings, kindness and inspiration in lending me to accomplish the book.

I want to express my gratitude to my parents for believing me. Also, I would like to thank my elder sister Grishma Ninave and my brothers Mrinal and Mangesh who have helped me with their valuable suggestions and guidance.

Further, I would express my special thanks to my extended family, my friends namely Sanskar, Priyanka and Tanushree for believing in me and helping me.

I am also thankful to Shubham Shah (Founder F&G) and Ishani Agrawal(Co-founder) and the whole Flairs and Glairs team who have given me the right platform.

Last but not least I would like to thank all the co-authors for all their co-operation.

-Nishita Ninave

Co Author

Shubham Shah (Founder, Flairs and Glairs)
Ishani Agarwal (Co-founder, Flairs and Glairs)
Grishma Ninave (Compiler)
Nishita Ninave (Co-compiler)

1. Somya Pandey
2. Garima Batra
3. Trisha Banerjee
4. Aiman Almas
5. Saloni Lal Srivastava
6. Arkapriya Ghosh
7. Swati Sharma
8. Victoria Trinidade
9. Avinash Kate
10. Tanuska Sarkar
11. Soumi Roy
12. Sampurna Ghosh
13. Dr Rakesh R Mund
14. Kanupriya Rastogi
15. Prachi Sharma
16. Avnish Kumar
17. Chirag L Sagar
18. Riya Reji Jacob
19. Faij Ahmad
20. Abilashni (A) Kamakshi Venkateswaran
21. Dr. Suryanka Singh
22. Madhura R J
23. Riya Rashmi Dash
24. Aishwarya Garg
25. Ruchika Shrikant Morghade

26. Siddharth Jain
27. Kashish Anand
28. Chetan Bhartiya
29. Sakshi Pandey
30. Nikeeta Sharma
31. Vrushali Khewale
32. Chirag Mehrotra
33. Rancey Jain
34. Divyanshi Nayan
35. Sriya Sri
36. Shivika Sharma
37. Ishant Nikure
38. Eshan Gupta
39. Yamini Sharma

Shubham Shah

(Founder- Flairs and Glairs)

Shubham Shah, an entrepreneur at "Flairs & Glairs" a brand with dynamics in events organizing and cultural educational pan INDIA, is a 26yrs old guy who recently has entered the digital platform of imprinting emotions. He has initiated with his own open mic platform to help budding poets and aspiring writers under his brand named as "Teekhe Zasbaaat"

He is a commerce graduate from the Bhagalpur City of Bihar. He states Writing has impersonated him since childhood and he has now been writing for over a decade!
Cooking, on the other hand, is his passion! He also mentions, trying out new things just tickles him!
When asked sir, Why SPICY EMOTIONS?
He smiled and added, "agar jasbaat teekhe na ho toh wo jasbaat kahan" Spices are all that blends! So do his words!
As a chef, he presents to you his dish! Hot and freshly served! Taste it! Feel it! Enjoy it! You can also find his writing in the Book "Teekhe Zasbaaat" and 50+ Co-authored anthologies.
With his passion to explore opportunities across Platforms, he is working with keen devotion and We wish him all the very best for his future ventures.
He is Featured in the **International Magazine De-Mode** for his upcoming solo novel.
He is **Approved by Ne8x for its Lit Fest,** and is a **Golden Star Awards 2020 Winner.**
He is an **India Book of Records Holder** for his Anthology **Satrang,** and has the **Grandmaster** title by **Asia Book of Records**, for the same.
He has also been featured in **Prabhat Khabar**, **Dainik Jagran** and other renowned Newspaper for his achievements. He has also been awarded with **India Star Republic Award 2021.**
He has been a proud co-author to
India Book of Records (Title- Black)
World Book of Records (Title -15 Wonders of Poetries)
India Book of Records (Title - Aaina)
Vajra World Records Holder (Title - Gustakhi Maaf Hai)
High Range of Records Holder (Title - Gustakhi Maaf Hai)

Share your reviews on his

INSTAGRAM
@spicy_emotions
@shubham4shah

Or via email on
shubham2shah@gmail.com

To stay tuned to his work and opportunities follow his business Handles

INSTAGRAM FACEBOOK YOUTUBE

@flairsandglairs
@teekhezasbaaat

WEBSITE:
https://flairsandglairs.in/
https://flairsandglairs.com/

Ishani Agarwal

(Co-Founder- Flairs and Glairs)

Ishani Agarwal hails from the City of Joy, Kolkata.
She is the co-founder of her Community "Teekhe Zasbaaat" and Flairs and Glairs Publication.
Been a Compiler for 45+ Anthologies, she is in the process for more. Co-authored in 150+ Anthologies. She is a India Book of Records Holder, a Vajra World Records Holder, a High Range of Records Holder and a Bravo Record holder.

Approved by Ne8x for its Lit Fest 2020, and Literary Icon 2020. Also a Golden Star Awards Winner 2020.
She has also been awarded with India Star Republic Award 2021.
She has been featured by the National Magazine "Taree Zameen Par" with the title 'unstoppable'.
Also featured in the International Magazine DeMode for her upcoming solo novel, she is proud to write on social issues, and is happy with the love she is receiving.
Connect with her on Instagram: @Ishani_agarwal_quotes / @compilations_so_far

Grishma Ninave

(Compiler)

A student of science and an admirer of arts from Nagpur, Maharashtra.
Currently working as a Project Head at Flairs and Glairs Publication House. Published in the Editorial section of a national magazine as Aaj Ki Womaniyaa, in the first edition of 2021.
A minion millennial with extra-large dreams.

Is in an active rebellion with her mother about the number of books she must have in the house. When not reading, can be found writing and reviewing books a lot.
A firm believer that music is what can revive and reconcile the world. She's one of those people who love greys more than colours and she's like colourful autumn too at the same time.
Admires old school love stories and retro music.
A Capricorn girl who believes hearts are more important than physical appearances. Is into deep talks with a very few people, but believes they are the driving force of joy in her life.
Loves travelling to places where there are mountains, trees, hills and treks.
No wonder nature's beauty strikes a chord within her.
The guiding light in her life is the quote, "Don't search for happiness, because it's not something you find, it's something you create!"

Has participated more than 150 anthologies and Compiled the Titles – Whispers of the Pen, Ansuni Aawaaz, Monika, The League, Sizzling Thoughts, Dil ki Dastaan, Grishm, Vijayant, Verge of Horizon and working on more.

Launched her first solo book titled “Jagriti – Awakening of the Soul” in December 2020.

E-mail – ninavegrishma@gmail.com
Instagram - @grish_ninave; @the_compiled_words

आदत सी कर ली

निगाहों ने निगाहों से
जब दोस्ती कर ली
हमने अपने दिल की राहें
प्यार से भर ली

मुस्कुराहटों के एहसास से
प्यार के दर्द तक
दिल ने खुद में
धड़कन सी भर ली

साथ चलते चलते
साथ छूट जाने तक
दिल ने अपनी मंज़िल
तय सी कर ली

सुबह शाम हाथ थामे
मोहब्बत के मोड़ पर
हमने उनके ना होने की
आदत सी कर ली

आत्महत्या! क्या यह एकमात्र समाधान है?

उम्मीद की किरान ढूँढते ढूँढते,
जब थकान महसूस होने लगती है,
दिल पूछता है,
आत्महत्या! क्या यह एकमात्र समाधान है?

जीने की वजह की तलाश में,
जब एक हार सी महसूस होती है,
दिल पूछता है,
आत्महत्या! क्या यह एकमात्र समाधान है?

लोगो की हँसी देख कर अपनी मुस्कान खोजते हुए,
जब एक घुटन सी महसूस होने लगती है,
दिल पूछता है,
आत्महत्या! क्या यह एकमात्र समाधान है?

सुबह उठ कर नज़र किसी प्यार करने वाले को ढूँढते हुए,
जब धुंधली सी महसूस होने लगती है,
दिल पूछता है,
आत्महत्या! क्या यह एकमात्र समाधान है?

When I Last Met You

The hangover of when I last met you
still ponders over my head.
Where the eyes were grave
but still conveyed what they were not meant to...

The Hangover of when I last met you
is like a thunderstorm I wish to get rid of.
Where so less was spoken
but so much was said...

The hangover of when I last met you
Confuses me like a jigsaw puzzle.
Where the eyes seem to smile
and the lips seem to cry...

The hangover of when I last met you
is like the red sky.
Where the Sun loses its existence
only to give way to the moon....

Dark

Come O' beloved
I want to hear you cry
Grab my hand cuz
That'll fix your broken pieces
Going away might
Fix it for you
But your absence has
Broken it all for us
Give me your energy
I'll give it back to you
Moulded into smiles
Give me your negativity
I'll give it back to you
Moulded into positivity
I know you see
Light far there
But I'll give you
The brightest light, I promise.
I know you see
Comfort far there
But I'll give you
The best comfort, I promise.
Back here, without you
Everything will be dark,
Everything will be dark...

Nishita Ninave

(Compiler)

Someone who is blessed with skills and art, Nishita is that combination of arts and science.A belief that helping others and being into philanthropic deeds, resides in her. She is co-author for more than 25+ books and also compiler of many books. Her work was published in a national magazine. Nishita believes that through writing one can express what he/she feels.

A belief that helping others and being into philanthropic deeds, resides in her.

She's found listening to silent music and trances most of the times.
She was not too much into literature since childhood, but poetry has been her solace in adulthood.
She believes penning down your feelings is the best way to express them, and it rekindles your soul. She has started compiling and also is co-author of more than 25 books.
Instagram handle- @heart_capturing

Somya Pandey

Somya Pandey is a medical doctor currently pursuing further studies in medicine. She started writing a few years ago during her MBBS, when she found herself in the grasp of depression. She found a means for expression in poetry then, and has never stopped writing since.

She is also working on her very first book, 'Caressing Monsters', a collection of poems from the dark times she faced during her college life. Make sure you check her work on Amazon, coming out soon!

You can find her on Instagram here:
@theselfdevelopmentjunkie

Soon

In moments I can't be there
I turn to moving screens
I know they can't replace me
Only sowing more unrest in my heart.

She's about to leave
And I'm not ready to grieve yet
Will I ever be?
Turns out love kills

I'm not packing any suitcases
I won't let go of her hand
I've braved many a storm in my young days
But this time I'm taking a stand

It feels like I'm a knight preparing for a war
I'm about to fight myself again
I'm about to close my heart forever
And seek my own demise in the mountains.

Vacant

Lightweight
is how I feel
Every night
When I miss his voice
Nightlights
Shimmer in my mind
At the thought
Of his smile
Heaviness
settles in
Soon after
I win my mind over
I end up
Watching movies
With broken lights
in my mind
Flowing into darkness
in the river.

Garima Batra

Garima has been a Journalism and Mass Communication student. She also has a Post-Graduation Diploma in Public Relations and has worked in the PR industry for three years. Presently, she is working as a freelance content writer and has been a co-author in approximately 50 anthologies. A bibliophile, a foodie and Sufi music lover, she loves to interact with people and build connections. She can be contacted at bgarima08@gmail.com or @thescribblersdais

Let Bygones Be Bygones

"It was just four days ago that I was talking to a friend and I got reminded of a person whom I never met but still has a place in my life. My friend said to me, '' Bhai always says me to go for long drives on weekends to relax and have some fun and I always refuse him."

And I immediately asked, "Why do you do so? Every freaking time?" I knew the reason for his refusal. He was extremely introverted and didn't like hanging out much. Rather at all. But he has a brother and what could have been better than this? To have some fun times with your elder brother who is ready to take you out.

He replied, "You know I am like this only. I snapped, '' Because you have a sibling you don't value. I know if I had a sibling and if he/she would have been elder to me, I would have eaten his head to take me out with him/her for lunch or dinner dates, trips, parties, etc. And had he/she been younger to me, I would have spoilt him/her. I would have taken my sibling out for trips and brunches and would have given him/her royal treatment."

I couldn't complete my sentence. I wanted to say I wish I had one with whom I could share my life, my mood swings, my achievements, a sibling bond. Technically, I did have one. But then my mother had to abort the child as the doctor informed her that it could be risky for her and the baby's life. There were many complications.

I know it must have been the toughest thing for her. To abort the child and to think about her and me. But the additional reason to take such a decision was my grandmother and family

conditions. My grandmother and my mom never got along. Not a single day went by when they did not fight. Raising me was tough in that disturbed environment along with a full-time job and household chores. Hence, my mother did not want to welcome another child and increase the chances of disturbances in the family.

I sometimes feel it's great that kid did not come into the world. Otherwise, he/she would have to live in an unhappy home, disturbed family, and grow up to be just like me, fighting every day for some peace and happiness.

However, I also imagine how different would my life have been had I had one. It would have been one hell of a roller-coaster ride.
I sometimes wonder what if my maternal grandparents, maternal uncle would have been alive? Had the situation been any different? Had the disturbances at my place lessened? Would I be having a sibling by my side? Would I have also got the privilege of going away for summer and winter vacations at Nani's place?

However, these are occasional thoughts and I have never let them affect my life. By God's grace, I have parents, cousins, and friends who are no less than a sibling. They have made me feel special in their own ways and supported me at every step. My wishes have been fulfilled, my troubles have been solved, my heartbreaks have been cured by them.

What I can't mend is my mom's, broken heart. I know she misses her parents, her brother, her sister, she somewhere feels terrible for having aborted the child. At times, she feels she is all alone. The only thing that keeps her going is me. She says I am her biggest achievement.

What else can one ask for? What I have cannot replace what I couldn't but indeed somewhere compensates for the bygone! The harsh reality is that we can't ever move on but we just keep shoving them aside and keep us distracted. We do forgive but we don't forget.

You can't share everything with every person on this earth. You ought to keep some things inside. But don't ever let it eat you up from the inside. What happened is in the past, the future is unpredictable. The present is what you have. You have the gift of life and you should embrace it. Cherish each moment of it. Take charge of what is in your hands and let go of the guilt of whatever happened and the anxiety of the present!
As Samuel Rutherford devised the correct usage of the phrase, 'let bygones be bygones!'

There was silence for a few seconds and then the hall was filled with the applause and hooting of the audience.
That was my time guys. Thank you for being a lovely audience.
Stay safe! Stay happy! Stay healthy!''

Khyati said as she climbed down the stage and left for the green room. She was nostalgic and shaking. This was her 10th show on a motivational speaking platform but every time recalling the same story gave her goosebumps. It reminded her what all her mother had to go through to ensure her survival. The girl who was motivating and inspiring everyone on the stage was in fact low and shook behind the curtains.

She removed her jacket and heels, washed her face, took some deep breaths and a few sips of water, and tried to calm herself down. Indeed being an influencer comes at a cost. And it ain't easy. But she was working on it and wanted to bring about a change in the thinking of the world, the condition of women and to break stereotypes.

“Ms. Khyati Kashyap, the media is waiting for you in the conference room. How much time do you require? We have to update them accordingly?”

“Please tell the organizers I need 5 minutes. I will be there.”, Khyati replied.

She then straightened her hair, touched up her makeup, wore her coat and slipped on her high heels, and stepped out with a vivacious and infectious smile, the brightest one could ever see, carrying on the ocean of turbulence inside but now shadowing her vulnerability with her confidence and smile.

Trisha Banerjee

Trisha Banerjee is a person who gives an equal weightage to her heart and brain and stands by the right decision in her life. She is a passionate, promising perfectionist. Music, food and dogs are her major turn ons. Keeping her dreams, her first priority she goes on in her life like an unstoppable storm.

The forever leading light- Sushant Singh Rajput (21st January, 1986-14th June ,2020)

Sushant Singh Rajput was a proficient, competent and talented actor, television personality, dancer and philanthropist. He died a mysterious death on 14th June, 2020 which send shockwaves not only throughout the country but also the entire world. As a student, he was focused and perspicacious. He initially pursued Mechanical Engineering as his career after he ranked seventh in DCE Entrance Exam. But he did not stop there. Rajput had high vaulting ambition and he dreamt of establishing himself as an actor. The Patna boy worked day and night to strike his goal. After gaining a huge fame working in two television blockbusters and two popular reality shows he finally made his Bollywood debut in the movie 'Kai Po Che' in 2013.With his amazing acting skills, he set the theatres on fire. He was a God-gifted person who through his versatility, capability and ingenuity gave twelve phenomenal films in his entire career to Indian Cinema. A man with an optimistic attitude knew how to live and enjoy every moment of his life. He believed either he should work hard then or never. His keen interest in astrophysics made stargazing one of his favourite activities. He was a man who loved reading books, writing and challenging himself with the impossible. Besides being an eminent actor, he was a sympathetic human being. He invested his money in child welfare centres and educational institutes. He treated the poor with commiseration and never felt any shame doing so. A very straightforward gentleman who stood by the right even if he was alone preaching it. A person who was not only recognized in India with awards but also had gained international fame and support. He was a staunch believer in God and followed the path of truth. We being his admirers should also follow his ideals. Where God showers his blessings, truth always prevails. Satyameva Jayate.

Aiman Almas

Aiman Almas is a passionate reader, amateur writer, animal lover, egalitarian, sarcastic on all occasions and in the midst of it all, a Doctor.
She's currently pursuing higher studies in medicine.
She is a fierce protector of the underdog, and will not rest until she has made their lives better. Her conviction inspires everyone around her. She believes in fighting until you've won.

You can find her on Mirakee @namia28.

Syria - The Lost Hope

I have a writer's block
I can't write.
Or think.
Or feel.
Nothing inspires me.
Or moves me so much
that I'm compelled to write.
My fingers have turned cold.
And numb.
Useless.
The futility of my being
The frivolousness of my existence hangs over me.

For whatever I write,
they will die.
They will be slaughtered.
They will bleed
and burn
and choke
to an early death.
My writings will reach them,
as much as a peace treaty does.
My prayers are already lost
in the smoke
from the burning homes.
And the charred bodies.
My tears will dry out under the blaring sun.
I wish there was something
I could do.
End the war,
And the senseless murders
Of innocent smiles

but I cannot
All I can wish for
Is to at least
have the strength
Of hoping against hope.

Saloni Lal Srivastava

She is Saloni Lal Srivastava daughter of Mr. Kumar Prashant and Mrs. Asha Sinha from Siwan, Bihar.
She is currently, working as a Project Coordinator under Flairs & Glairs Publication House.
And also, purchasing B.sc in Botany honours.
Her life is all around her family, friends and career.
She has also worked as co-author in 30+ anthologies. She is the one who loves to spread smile and positivity to everyone.
You can follow her on Instagram: @salonilalsrivastava.

प्रिय अंकित,
मेरी सबसे छोटे, सबसे प्यारे भाई। आज ये ख़त तुझे लिख रही हूं। अपने दिल की बात बयां करने के लिए मुझे यह तरीका अपनाना पड़ेगा कभी सोचा नहीं था। आज हमारी दुनिया अलग है। तू उस दुनिया में और मैं इस दुनिया में। तुझे पता है 15 जनवरी 2004 को जब तू इस दुनिया में आया था मानो हमारी जिंदगी में बाहर से आ गई थी। जैसे ही मुझे ख़बर मिली मैं तुझे मिलने को तुझे अपने इस गोद में लेने को बेचैन हो उठी थी। पता है घर से तेरे पास आने के बीच रास्ते में मैं बस एक ही बात सोचती रही थी। आखिर में अपने इस नन्हीं सी जान को किस नाम से बुलाऊंगी और पूरे रास्ते हजारों नाम सोच डाले। फिर अंत में एक नाम पर आकर रुकी और वह नाम था अंकित। फिर क्या था मेरी ज़िद घरवालों को माननी पड़ी और तेरा नाम अंकित पड़ गया। मेरी खुशी का कोई ठिकाना ना था। अब मेरे दो नहीं तीन छोटे भाई थे, जो इस दुनिया के सबसे प्यारे भाई थे। फिर क्या था मुझे अब तुझसे मिलने का बस बहाना चाहिए था। इधर मेरी छुट्टियां शुरू नहीं होती थी कि मैं तेरे पास पहुंच जाती थी। मानो हमारी जिंदगी खुशियों से भर गई थी। हम जब भी मिलते हजारों बदमाशियां करते, खूब मस्ती करते। वक्त के साथ-साथ हमारी छोटी बहनें भी आई पर सबसे छोटा भाई तो तू ही रहा। तुझे याद है हम जब भी मिलते थे, कितना मस्ती करते थे। किसी खेत से गन्ने चुराने हो या घर में बिन बताए कहीं भी घूमने निकल जाना हमने खूब किया। हम सब भाई बहनों में तेरा निशाना सबसे खटीक था। याद है हमें जब भी पेड़ से आम तोड़ना होता था सब पेड़ पर चढ़ते या निशाना लगाने की नाकाम कोशिश करते पर तू नीचे ही खड़ा एक बार में कई आम तोड़ डालता था। हम सब जितना ज्यादा हल्ला करने वाले तू उतना ही शांत रहने वाला था। हम सब से बिल्कुल ही उल्टा था तू पर हम सब के

साथ मस्तियां करने में भी पीछे नहीं रहता था। जब भी घर में पूरा परिवार इकट्ठा होता तो तू बैट लेकर पहुंच जाता था। कहता चलें सब क्रिकेट खेलें और हम सब ना नहीं कर पाते फिर सब क्रिकेट खेलते। पता है बाबू आज ना जान क्यों तेरा बिताया हर वो पल इन आंखों के सामने घूम रहा है। तुझे याद है जब हम वैष्णो देवी जाने के लिए पठानकोट आए थे तो तू कितना खुश हुआ था। मानो तुझे कोई खज़ाना मिल गया हो। हम तकरीबन 10 दिन वहां रुके और इन 10 दिनों में ना जाने इतनी यादें बना ली। हमारा वो साथ में अमृतसर जाना तो बाघा बॉर्डर घूमना। हमारा वो वैष्णो देवी जाना तो पांडव गुफा घूमना। मानो वे दिन मेरी जिंदगी में तेरे साथ बिताए सबसे बेहतरीन दिन थे। वैष्णो देवी की चढ़ाई करने से ठीक पहले तुझे बुखार हो गया था। हम सबके मना करने के बाद भी तुम्हें चढ़ाई की थी। हमने वहां इतनी सारी यादें बनाई जिन्हें इस खत में लिखना मानो नामुमकिन सा है। याद है बाबू अमृतसर में जब हम सामान खरीद रहे थे तो सब आगे निकल गए। मैं और तू बस पीछे थे क्योंकि मुझे कड़ा लेना था और मेरे हाथों के नाप का नहीं मिल रहा था। तब तूने ही दुकान में से ढूंढ कर निकाला था। आज भी वह कड़ा मेरे हाथों में है। वक्त बीतता गया हमने हजारों यादें बनाई। पर कहते हैं जब कोई बहुत खुश होता है तो ऊपर वाले से उसकी खुशियां नहीं देखी जाती। शायद यही हुआ हमारे साथ है भी। वक्त का सिक्का कुछ युं पलटा कि हम सबकी जिंदगी में अंधेरा लेकर आया। फिर हमारे जिंदगी का वो काला दिन भी आ गया जिस दिन मेरा सबसे छोटा सबसे प्यारा भाई यानी कि तू हम सब को छोड़कर चला गया। 1 अगस्त 2020 की रात मैं यह सोचकर कि सुबह उठ कर सबको खुशखबरी दूंगी कि मेरी कविताएं और कहानियां 1 नहीं 5 किताबों में एक साथ छपी है पर होनी को कुछ और ही मंजूर था। मुझे नहीं पता था कि सुबह

जब मेरी आंखें खुलेगी तो मेरे चेहरे पर किताब छपने की खुशी नहीं बल्कि आंखों में सिर्फ दर्द और आंसु होंगे। वह 2 तारीख मेरी जिंदगी का काला दिन बन जाएगा। मेरा छोटा मुझे हमेशा के लिए छोड़ कर चला जाएगा। मुझे माफ करना बच्चे मैं आखिरी वक्त में तेरे साथ नहीं रह पाई। मुझे पता है तू मेरी आस पास ही है।तू हमें रोता नहीं देख सकता पर क्या करें हम लाख कोशिश करने के बावजूद अपने आंसुओं को रोक नहीं पाते। तू हमेशा हमेशा हमारे दिलों में रहेगा। तेरे साथ बिताए हर वह पल हमारे जेहन में जिंदा रहेंगे। आज यह ख़त कितनी हिम्मत जुटा के लिख रही हूं बता भी नहीं सकती। मेरे आंसू आंखों से निकलने पर मजबूर हो गए है। मुझे माफ करना बच्चे कि मैं रो रही हूं। अब बस हर पल यही दुआ रहती है कि तू जहां भी हो खुश हो। बस एक ही बात कहुंगी बाबू तू लौट के आजा तेरे बिना यहां सब अधूरे है। बहुत याद आती है तेरी बाबू बहुत याद आती है।

तुझे याद करती,
तेरी तन्नु दीदी

Arkapriya Ghosh

"Numbing the pain for a while will make it worse when you finally feel it." Arkapriya Ghosh is an aspirant writer of myth, fantasy and solitude. From the age of 10 she loves literature and regards J K Rowling as her ideal. She has faced a lot of hardships from all sides, but
finds peace from all these by writing and reading. She finds solace in books amidst all worries and troubles.

Infinite Love

PROLOGUE:

“And we can see contestant number 7 leading the marathon, and SHE WINS” applause fills the whole stadium as I look all around. I find my elder sister's enemies shrieking in delight. Drops of tears escaped my cheeks as I shouted out in defeat as I realised, I couldn't fulfil my sister's dream.

I wake up with a jolt on the bed, my heart thumping vigorously." Tomorrow is a big day for me “I told myself and tried to sleep. Yet my thoughts drifted towards my sister as I found her portrait on the wall.

5 YEARS BACK:

It was just the day before Christmas. I was asleep deeply. Slowly my sister Aisha crept up to me and asked me "Will I win tomorrow’s marathon" I responded with sleepy eyes "Yes you will. Now please sleep." I tossed on the other side of bed and reminisce about my sister's struggle to take part in the marathon. My sister, Aisha isn’t that sort of a sporty girl. She didn't have much of a talent. She was just a good soul. However, when her school mates insulted her saying she was good-for-nothing she got desperate to win the marathon. She even had got into a bet with her friend, the famous athlete, Shreya that if she doesn't win the marathon, she will be their servant for a day.

On the day of Christmas eve, we went towards the orient stadium to see her race. We went into the spectator stand on wishing her good luck. The first race was a 100 metres race, and with great energy, Aisha won the match. However, at the time of Marathon when we saw all the participants on the field,

we couldn’t see Aisha. When we went to search for her, we saw that she had committed suicide. We were unable to believe it. While drops of tears cascaded my cheeks, i saw a note on my sister's bag. The note read

DEAR PRIYA,

I WANTED TO WIN THE MATCH DESPERATELY. I KNEW I WOULD WIN. HOWEVER SOMEONE HAD PUT BROKEN GLASSES IN MY SHOES. I CAN'T RUN. I WANT YOU TO FULFIL MY DREAM OF WINNING MARATHON AND DEFEATING SHREYA.
I QUIT.

PRESENT DAY:

I went to the Orient Stadium for the competition on the day of the Christmas eve. I also saw Shreya Di in the race. But I knew what to do. I had to run with the hope of fulfilling my sister's wish. I ran as I never could. I slowly overtook all contestants and won the race. When I looked up, I felt my sister's presence around me. Just then a gust of wind, tickled my ear as if to say "I was always here”. I smirked with the trophy in my hand. The day had barely begun.

Swati Sharma

Swati Sharma is a budding writer and can be usually found with her pen and diary in nature's lap. Ever since childhood she has been fond of writing poems and now, she is giving wings to her writings. Otherwise she is a sales professional in IT industry. Swati is a big foodie, loves to connect with people, loves sketching and enjoys riding her Avenger 220. She lives in Noida with her creativity and solitude. She can be found at https://www.instagram.com/ehsaas_the_words_unspoken/

The Memory Lane

Walking down the memory lane,
I found you and me,
Playing at the backyard
Beneath that mango tree,
Smiling from ear to ear
and being so carefree...

Walking down the memory lane
I found you and me
Picking up the fights
Then calming like a sea,
we were best of friends
just like Tom & Jerry

Walking down the memory lane
I found you and me
Singing loud in the rain
And dancing in the streets,
Jumping in the muddy puddles
And hurting our knees

Walking down the memory lane
I found you and me
You were wrapped in shroud
I was crying silently,
Leaving me behind
You were on your journey quietly...

Waking down the memory lane
I found you and me......

Your Wish is My Command

And then he cracked some known jokes,
to kill the awkward silence.
She chuckled like she used to,
& he gazed at her like he used to.
He then handed over in silence,
A piece of a forgotten memory they once shared.
She clenched it
in the palm of her hands
to gain courage
As she watched his life
leaving his body
one breath at a time
It was an episode
soaked in broken hopes
and incessant tears
A complete emotion
with an incomplete ending!

She silenced the chaos
in her head by yelling out aloud.
But don't waves crash?
Against the rocks with a roar?
Force of nature for the wave
Force of habit for her.

Victoria Trinidade

She is passionate about writing. She has keen interest in English Literature & Psychology. If words would be people, they would be her best friends. Her association with writing dates back to a decade and a half. Her intention is to share her perspective on feelings, events & occasions. The world is her canvas and her words, the brushstrokes.

A packet of Biscuits & A 20 Rupee Note

Like for every daughter in the world, my father was my superhero too. I almost felt invincible to all the problems just because he was always there for me. A man who taught me to live with integrity even when things went downhill. I have such fond memories of him. Then one fine day, as fate would have it, the fairy bubble I lived in was busted. He left us and what was worse is that he left me to figure out how to live on my own. For some unexplainable reason I just couldn't feel the grief. I think I knew this was the best thing that could happen to him. I know you just raised an eyebrow reading that, but I'd be lying if I felt otherwise after watching him suffer for 8 years under diabetes & immobility. And that's when I let go of my selfish ways.

I have uncountable reasons to be proud of him, but there is particularly one fond memory that I am going to share with all of you. Diabetes not only makes you vulnerable, it can make you cranky, very cranky. He experienced that too. The day he was diagnosed with it, I remember that look on his face. He was very scared. I can't be sure whether he was scared of the physical challenges that he was about to suffer or whether it was to see us helpless.

But nothing could curb his undying spirit. He was a fighter, one who could tackle almost anything with a smile. That spirit of his was so contagious! Naturally he spent most of his time indoors, mostly staring outside the door when he was alone. When asked, would just shudder his shoulder and say " Mrs. Tiwari is beautiful, I'm sure your mother won't mind if I tried woo her! He just quickly hid his helplessness under naïve humour.

One afternoon, as I was administering his usual dose of insulin, he asked me "Am I still your superhero?". I looked at him, held his hands assumingly and smiled. "Yes" I said very confidently. As a child I ran to him for everything that caught my attention. It could be a bar of white milky bar, an encyclopaedia or a funskool jigsaw puzzle, anything! All those memories suddenly flashed my mind and I thought to myself how exactly could I still make him feel that he was the same person who I ran to with my never-ending list of demands. So, I said that I want to have a packet of good-day biscuits that costed around five rupees. So, he reached out to his wallet with his trembling hands and removed a 20 rupees note and gave it to me and said, go buy what you want.

Those twenty rupees were priceless, I mean nothing in this world could match up to its value. He just made me fall in love with his innocence, trust me there is no greater love than that. Every Thursday he would habitually call me and hand over a twenty rupee note and I was equally excited to receive it. That was his way of letting me know that I was still his little girl.

As time passed by, his health started deteriorating. His condition grew worse. Year 2014, the year that changed my life forever. Dad left us. In the last ten minutes of his life he wanted to see me, I was told and I was not at home. Maybe he wanted to say something and now there is no way I will ever know what it is that he wanted to tell me. As he lay lifeless in our living room, I stood miserable staring at him. That feeling cannot be described. I walked up to him and rested my head on his chest and I couldn't hear his heartbeats or feel the warmth of his embrace. Trust me when I say this, I can trade anything in this world that I possess to hear his heart beat again. I couldn't do anything, absolutely nothing. At that moment, I slipped a twenty rupees note in his pocket and whispered in his hear that he has taken a part of my soul with him. And it is never coming back.

Today too, when my family visits his grave, I don't. I just sit on his chair, staring outside the same door with a packet of biscuit in my hand. That was our moment and it will always be that way. My purpose of sharing this episode was to relive the essence of the most awesome man I came across in my life. I know daddy is somewhere up there watching me as I type this. He knows that I think of him and we will always have this unique way of connecting with each other.

I don't know where you are, but wherever that is, you are not too far from me. My bundle of joy will always be the same packet of biscuit and that twenty rupees note. These memories is what is left of him with me and that is my most prized possession. Life may be timebound but my love for him knows no bounds. He lives in me even today, even today he sees the world but through my eyes. I will forever be indebted towards his endless love and sacrifice.

Avinash Kate

Avinash is an engineer by profession but he is a very good writer & photographer by passion. He not just writes a poem, he lives it.

Instagram ID: @ak_immortal_soul

बाप आठवत होता...

आज पुन्हा त्याचा कंठ दाटून आला होता,
आठवणींचा झरा डोळ्यातून वाहत होता,
बापच्या उशाशी बसून एक एक रात्र जागला होता,
आज पुन्हा त्याला त्याचा बाप आठवत होता...

आज पुन्हा तिचा ऊर भरून आला होता,
लेकीची हरवलेली प्रत्येक वस्तू बाप शोधून देत होता,
वस्तू शोधून देणारा तिचा बापच हरवला होता,
आज पुन्हा तिला तिचा बाप आठवत होता...

आज पुन्हा आयुष्यात तो थोडा खचला होता,
बापासारखा तो ही मेहनत घेत होता,
पण मेहनतीचं कौतुक करणारा बाप जवळ नव्हता,
आज पुन्हा त्याला त्याचा बाप आठवत होता...

पुन्हा तिचा जीव तीळ तीळ तुटत होता,
संसाराचा भार तिच्या एकली वर पडला होता,
ह्या रुक्मिणीचा विठ्ठल आता कायमचा रुसला होता,
आज पुन्हा तिला तिच्या लेकरांचा बाप आठवत होता...

आज पुन्हा त्यांना त्यांचा बाप आठवत होता...

बाबा...

रात्री गाढ झोपेत असताना अचानक
मध्येच अशी जाग येते,
बाबा तुझ्या असण्याची चाहूल
मध्येच कुठेतरी भासते.
बाबा तुझं वागणं, तुझं बोलणं
आम्हाला आमच्यातच कुठेतरी दिसतं,
बाबा वसलाय तू आमच्यातच तेव्हा कुठे जाणवतं,
सगळं विसरता आलं तरी
तुझं जाणं विसरता येत नाही,
पण खरं सांगू बाबा,
तुझ्याविना आयुष्याचा सूर मात्र
आता गवसत नाही...

Tanuska Sarkar

Student. Loves the sky. Mostly, trying to find the reason for her existence.

Left

If tears could build a staircase,
If memories would be a lane,
If I hadn't let go,
If unsaid words could be spoken,
I would do it all over again.
I stand alone, in the fields,
Where we once used to play,
Feel the wind whisper through the trees,
Search for answers that I'd missed.
The once green grass is no longer so,
Dew drops no longer form on them,
The fields are parched,
The petrichor no longer calms my soul.
The summer's long gone,
The same rains that drenched us
With memories for an entirety,
Are embers on my skin now.
The spring is almost departing,
The gerberas are no longer gay,
The wind gives me chills,
The skies have turned grey.
As autumn crept in,
The breezes began to blow,
Greenery, and my happiness,
Lulled themselves to sleep;
The bright leaves fell fast, and slow.
When I stood at the edge of the fields one last time,
It was winter -
Fog hung in the air,
The sky was dark,
The ground, white;
For once, I felt at peace,

On that lonely, cold wintry night.
As I turned to leave,
The memories came flooding back,
No longer could I hold back the tears,
That had been welling up inside.
I cried, and cried,
Till it no longer hurt,
The tears subsided,
The pain ceased to exist.
I walked back home, with new hope,
Death wasn't in our hands,
But life was,
Your loss resulted in me losing myself too.
However, when I ran to the fields next summer,
The grass was green, and fresh,
I was moved to tears to feel the breeze,
That beside your grave blew.

Soumi Roy

Soumi Roy, a mere 16-year-old teenager, born and brought up in the City of Joy, Kolkata has a unique way of expressing her emotions through writing. A firm believer that life isn't about finding yourself but all about creating yourself. Apart from writing, dance is also her favourite hobby

You Left Us Too Soon!

As a woman you by being my first child was the most heavenly thing I could have ever get. Me and your dad counted each day and felt your mischiefs inside me which were some ecstatic moments. You finally arrived on a one fine day by being the sunlight of our lives. We named you "Aurora" means "dawn of the early morn". I felt your breath close to mine and your doll like hands holding my fingers. But we did not know that you weren't meant to be with us for long. You left us silently emptying our whole coming life. I was shattered into million pieces and shouted your name a thousand times, hoping you would wake up from your never-ending sleep. But you didn't. Death is a nefarious thing on human life, but I believe you were no human but an angel of our life gifted as a drop of bliss. Yet am scratched with a never fading wound and forever numbness in my heart too guilt to not being able to let you experience what the world had to offer. But darling I promise you were, are and forever will be the dawn of my life without which my life won't witness any morning. I will always remember your winsome face which resembled mine and you will always be the permanent and rarest diamond of my life irreplaceable by anyone. I love you.
-Mama.

Sampurna Ghosh

18 years old, class 12 student, lives in West Bengal, Kolkata, likes to write poems, songs, stories, bad at "people".

Stolen from A Dream

I often find my head thrown back with laughter
at strangers' jokes,
and even in hysteria, I fear you storming into the room, asking me,
"What is so funny? You said you can't survive without me",
Yes.
It isn't funny that I dreamt of you last night,
stuck in that clumsy classroom with the noisy fans and flickering tube lights,
The class schedule, in your handwriting, on the bulletin.
The smell of ink and sweat and chalk lingered in class six B
And, you were still sitting next to me, obviously.
When I said "I can't survive without you",
And you replied with a "you bloody liar",
Even though, we both secretly knew
that we were each other's bridesmaid,
First aid
Band mate.
(Our band was supposed to be called "The Royal Flush")
Stamping nicely polished shoes,
My ponytail, askew, because of you.
You are still eleven, you were still eleven
But in my dream, I was of present age.
And I enlightened you with my five years latest news,
How I passed my boards with a one direction song...
stuck in my head in the examination hall.
How I've bought a guitar, and still can't play it,
How I've bought a new phone and my favourite tv series have changed.
And all the new embarrassing songs I've written about dating movie stars.
You stared at me, with your funny eyes and weird birthmarks,

Too detailed to be true.
And then I realized.
That this was a dream,
Because you smiled at me rather than slapping me down to the floor,
Because Mrs Ray didn't switch our seats for chatting in the physics class.
CAN I STEAL YOU FROM THIS DREAM?
NO.
The bell rang,
The last bell of the day,
Which meant us dashing out of the class, skating through the corridors, reaching home, watching YouTube videos, and googling assignment answers
But this time,
The bell resonated through the room
As the ceiling gave way to a pouring rain,
and washed you away.
And I am sorry that I woke up and Here I am,
my head thrown back with laughter at strangers' jokes,
and if you storm into the room, asking me questions,
I shall tell you
I lied,
When I said, "I can't survive without you"...
You're not my bridesmaid,
My first aid, my bandmate,
The fifth wall is your new best friend,
But I did survive,
Even though, right now,
A house fly,
A loud advertisement leaflet,
A car tyre dust particle,
Has more of a right to be around me
Than you will have, ever again.

Dr Rakesh R Mund

Dr Rakesh R Mund has been participating in more than 100 anthology and his solo books are ishq-e-panhi & Vidhwansh available on amazon, flifpkart and others platform. He read veda and different literatures which give a glimpse on his writing. You can contact with him : Instagram- @Rakeshmundr_

यार मेरा

नैनों से दूर तुम खो गये
यार तुम कहाँ चले गये ।
एक बंधन ऐसा अतुट था
जिंदगी में साथ तेरा उत्कृष्ट था ।।

पानी बहता था पहले खुशी से
अभी बहता तेरे यादों में खामोशी से ।
तु जब होता था एक रूआब अलग था
जो देखे थे साथ मिलके ख्वाब अलग था ।।

तुट कर बिखर गये हम तेरे जाने से
चली गई और एक जहाँ में पाने से ।
तु ईश्वर का प्यार बनगई मुझे छोड़कर
वादा किया था तुने चली वादा तोड़कर ।।

अनंत व्रह्माण्ड से ज्यादा था प्यार मेरा
इतनी ज्वाला सी चमक थी यार मेरा ।
इस जनम के आधे अधुरी मिलन दरार तेरा
अगले जनम फिर से मिलेंगे आना यार मेरा ।।

Kanupriya Rastogi

She is Kanupriya Rastogi from Bareilly UP
#दुआएं होती है मुकम्मल माक़ूल वक़्त पर,
जानती हूं खुदा पर यकीं और दिल में सब्र रखती हूं,
दुश्वारियां कितनी भी हों राहों में,
मैं अपनी मंज़िल पे नज़र रखती हूं,
और इन तीर - ओ - तलवार की दरकार ही नहीं मुझे प्रिया!!
मैं शायर हूं कलम की नोक पर दुनिया को झुकाने का हुनर रखती हूं.........

दादी मां

यूं तो घर में सभी प्यार करते हैं,
पर वो जिन्होंने बचपन से मुझे सबसे ज़्यादा प्यार दिया,
वो मेरी दादी मां थीं।
जब वो थीं तो बहुत मस्त थी ज़िन्दगी अपनी भी,
न कोई काम न कोई चिंता,
जो मेरे हिस्से के सारे काम भी खुद ही कर लिया करती थीं,
बिना कुछ किए भी अगर शाम को उनके पास लेट जाऊं,
तो बहुत प्यार से पूछती थीं,
कैसे थक गया बच्चा मेरा, आजा मैं तेरे पांव दबा दूं,
पर उनके जाने के बाद न तो वो झूठ मूठ कि थकान का एहसास होता है न ही उस सच्चे वाले प्यार का,
हमेशा मुझे डांटने वालों की जो डांट लगाती थीं,
वो मेरी दादी मां थीं।
उनके साथ अपने बचपन का मैंने खूबसूरत वक़्त बिताया था,
और आज भी शरारतों पर मेरी मां कहती हैं मुझसे,
कि, इसकी दादी ही तो थीं जिन्होंने इसको सबसे ज़्यादा सर चढ़ाया था,
मेरे मन की बात वो अक्सर बिना कहे भी जान लेती थीं,
मेरी हर बेतुकी ज़िद भी वो घर में सबसे ज़्यादा आसानी से मां लेती थीं,
मेरी मुस्कुराहटों से खिल उठता था हर दफा चेहरा उनका,
मेरी हर उदासी तो जैसे उनकी जान लेती थी,
सच कहूं अगर तो मेरी खुशियों का वो चलता फिरता मुकम्मल जहां थीं.........
वो मेरी दादी मां थी।
मेरी हर शैतानी को जिन्होंने मेरी मां से भी ज़्यादा सहा,
और फिर भी सबसे ज़्यादा मुझसे प्यार किया,
अपने आखरी लम्हों में भी वो बस मेरा नाम लेती रहती थीं,

अपनी नज़रों से मुझे एक पल को भी दूर नहीं जाने देती थीं,
वो मेरी दादी मां थीं।
आज भी यूं तो जीने में कोई कमी नहीं है,
मगर फिर भी कभी जब आज मैं उदास होती हूं ,
तो सबसे ज़्यादा जो खलती है वो बस उनकी ही कमी है,
कि आज जब कभी मिलता है कोई सम्मान या कामयाबी तो,
खुश होकर देने को आशीर्वाद सबके साथ मेरी दादी मां अब नहीं हैं,
ज़िन्दगी से दूर सही पर दिल में हमेशा उतना ही करीब होंगी,
वो जितना बचपन में करीब थीं,
क्योंकि वो मेरी दादी मां थीं..........
वो मेरी दादी मां थीं।।

Prachi Sharma

Prachi Sharma is a writer who likes to write her feelings in her unique sort of way. She participated in more than 15 anthologies as a co-author. She likes to play kabaddi. She likes teddy bears, chocolates , singing and Dancing. She likes to read motivational, fiction and romantic books. She is a Founder of KAVYANJALI. She is dreamer and achiever and she believes she deserves to be successful and she is best in her way.

कह दे कोई

मन बेचना है मेरा
आखें तलाश रही है!
खबर ये जो आई है !
कह दे कोई, सच नहीं !

दिल मेरा घबरा रहा है!
हाथ - पैर मेरे फूल रहे हैं!
दिमाग मेरा बदं हो गया!
कह दे कोई, सच नहीं!

इस खबर ने तो,
मार दिया है मुझे भी!
कह दे कोई, मज़ाक है ये सब
वापस आ जाओ कही से,
साबित कर दो झूठा, ये खबर जो आई है!

यकीन दिला रही हूँ ,मैं सबको
कि लौट के तुम आओगे!
जो वादा तुम ने किया है!
पूरा करने तुम आओगे!

जब लाश तुम्हारी लाए थे!
मर गयी थी, मैं भी उस दिन
टूट गया था हर वादा,
टूट गया था हर वो सपना,

बदं करो अब, ये नातक अपना
डर गई हूँ, अब मैं भी,

अब उठ जा ना भाई,
कह दे ना, मज़ाक था ये

बोल दे खुद ही,
बहन पहले की तरह, ये मज़ाक था!
अब तो उठ जा ना भाई,
बंद कर ना, ये नातक अपना

न जाने ये खबर,
क्यो अब ये सच - सी लग रही है!
जो तुझे चाहिए ना, वो ला दूंगी मैं
बंद कर ना, ये नातक अपना

कह दे कोई,
खामोश लेता है, ये पागल.
ये पागल का नातक है!

Avnish Kumar

A resolute recluse, Avnish is an anachronistic soul.
He is a voracious reader, aspiring author and has a momentous dream of owning as many books as humanly possible.
A chemistry teacher professionally, he lives his life through his other hobbies of writing, music, bhangra and avoiding as many social gatherings as possible.
He is also fond of rhymes and loves reading and writing shayaris. He has an immaculate love for learning new languages and is currently on his way to explore Urdu.

माँ और मैं

कभी मिल तो तुझको बताऊं मैं
तुझे इस तरह से सताऊं मैं
तुझे पकड़ूं एक पल ज़ोर से
तेरी गोद में सो जाऊं मैं।

तू देखे मुझको प्यार से
तुझे फिर गले से लगाऊं मैं
तू हाल मुझसे पूछ ले
और फिर से हिचकिचाऊं मैं।

तेरे पास बैठूं इस तरह
तुझे सारे किस्से सुनाऊं मैं
फिर तू कहे और मैं सुनूं
बस तुझको सुनता जाऊं मैं।

तुझे ले चलू रसोई में
फिर पराठे बनवाऊं मैं
तुझे दो कहूं तू चार सुने
और छह के छह खा जाऊं मैं।

तू आना फिर दरवाज़े पे
जब दूसरे शहर जाऊं मैं
मुझे मुठ्ठी बंद कर पैसा दे
जिन्हें फिर गले से लगाऊं मैं।

तू पूछे घर कब आएगा
और फिर बहाना बनाऊं मैं
तू मुझसे फिर से रूठना

और तुझको फिर से मनाऊं मैं।

अगर तू है पानी झील का
तो किनारे एक पौधा हूं मैं
जो तू है तो पूरा एक हूं
जो तू नहीं तो आधा हूं मैं।

जो मैं हूं राही खुदा का
तो तू मेरा मज़ार है
जो तू नहीं तो कुछ नहीं
जो तू है तो सब गुलज़ार है।

मैं तैर के आ जाऊंगा
जो तू नदी के पार है
मेरा जो सही सब तू ही है
मेरा बाकी सब बेकार है।

Chirag L Sagar

Chirag L Sagar is a 1st year MBBS student studying at Srinivas Institute of Medical Sciences and Research Centre, Mangalore. His hobbies are poetry, reading - books, novels, autobiographies, philately, listening to songs, sports like cricket and badminton, cooking. He is a medico by profession and a writer by passion. His dream is to become an Oncologist and a successful writer.

Instagram : @chirag_cls18 Facebook : Chirag LSagar

An Unsent Letter To Heaven

Reminiscing all the fun,
And good times we've had together.
Here's a heartfelt note,
To the one who inspired me,
To become who I am, today.
Three years since you left me forever,
I've been through a lot.
My life had become a total mess,
And still is !
All those wonderful moments we spent together,
All those futile talks to lame jokes,
Making infinite memories.
With both of us having the same goal in life,
While you leaving me behind midway,
Everything has changed a lot.
You made me who I am today,
Boy I'll be grateful to you forever.
The last movie we watched together,
Seems your dream of meeting SSR someday,
has become a reality in your case.
A never-ending nightmare struck me,
On my 17th birthday,
When you wished me luck and left me alone, forever.
Hope you're doing great wherever you are !
The world has become a lot more cruel,
From the day we parted ways.
But now,
Everyday I wake up with a smile,
With the belief that you're looking upon me.
Thanks for the innumerable times of help, support and encouragement,
Just to see an infectious laughter on my face.

Your unheard dreams and wishes,
Will be fulfilled by your best friend,
Of whom, you'll always be proud.
Here's to wishing you lots of love, good health
With truckloads of happiness.
I miss you every passing day,
But there's someone in my life,
Who never makes me realize your absence.
Hope we meet each other someday,
To have many more memories.
Here I am, signing off.
Thank you for everything, may you be blessed with eternal happiness.

Riya Reji Jacob

Riya Reji Jacob is a 22 yr old writer from Bhopal who is currently pursuing MBBS and started penning at the age of 11. She's peppy , scrupulous and likes to keep it simple yet significant as she believes that the right words are always simple. She has co-authored over 80 anthologies and aims to inspire people through her writings. Apart from writing she loves to sing, sketch and play piano.

Yaad Hai Mujhe

Woh chipte chipate apka mishri dena
dusro se humesha...thoda zyada;
koi baat hojane pe pyar se samjhana
yaad hai mujhe....

bin maange, maa se chipkar
gullak me chillar dena
aur "koi bhi zarurat ho mujhe batana" kehna...
yaad hai mujhe!

Woh meri har zidd pe mera saath dena
aur mere liye maa - papa ko manana,
Waqt bhale hi kum mila saath
par jo mila , woh kitna zaruri tha...
ehsaas hai mujhe.

Waqt badal gaya hai
aur saath badal gaye kayi rishte;
Achcha hai yeh badlav apke rehte nhi hua,
khoon ka rishta bhool gaye log...
raste huye yu alag,
ke kahi toh insaniyat ne bhi keh diya - alvida!

Yaad karti hu aaj bhi aap dono ko
apki baaton ko, unn yaadon ko...
Nana - Nani shayad apse kaha nhi kabhi
par shukriya... choti choti cheeze sikhane ko.

Yaad toh hai ki kaise ek pal me
chhod gaye aap log,
par socha toh maine bhi tha aasuo me apko bhulana nahi hai mujhe;

lagta hai jaise kal hi ki baat hai...
lagta hai jaise kal hi ki baat hai...
jab pyar se paas bulate the aap mujhe.

Woh dusro se thoda zyada -
chipkar mujhe mishri dena ....
Woh maa ko bin bataye
gullak me chillar dena,

Yaad hai mujhe!!
Yaad rahega - humesha.

Faij Ahmad

He is trainee navigational officer cadet. He has co-authored 10+ books and compiled one book. He is bit into academics and equally on ground. You can connect him on Instagram @shibbuahmed

Crumbled Heart, Shed No Tears

Sunken instance tried but couldn't choke me. I pose soft and streamline in public. But the heart of iron has got electrifying ions. I swim, I never sink. That instance was worth sinking but the curves of my body resisted without lifebuoy. After a big year, I reached home at 8:30 with a load of heavy joy on my face. My eyes assembled everyone but she was missing. I didn't ask but my calibre realized the fact. Eyes wanted to whisper tears but I didn't let it. My soul soaked in silence started searching, I marched every room, every corner. Walls, her bowl, that missing fragrance swept all illusion and narrated full story. While unlacing my shoe, my disturbed mental peace assured: "she is no more". Even after sticking to all truth, my heart didn't acknowledge the fact. My soul cried out of innocence and I called my sister to a little cornered storeroom. To rely on my courtesy, I asked: " where is she?". With her soft voice, she added, "Nanna is no more".

I pretended to give a short, sharp smile by patting her back I said: " it happens, the sad truth of life". Those electrifying ions compelled me not to weep and I started behaving as if it is normal. After taking food with everyone, I came back to bed. I had never thought that night will hang this much high on me. My eyes and pillow had some conversation and I slept.

Abilashni (A) Kamakshi Venkateswaran

Abilashni (A) Kamakshi Venkateswaran
Graduated from Computer Science, She is into Software Industry for the past 7 years. Writing and journalism was always in her bucket list, rain or shine! She started developing her interest in writing on 11th class, after being bored on concept of Integral Calculus!

Becoming Inariculate In Your Thoughts

How inarticulate we become, every time when we see our friend's mobile displaying as "Dad calling". Yes! It has been 13 years, and now I am fortunate enough to emote my inner self, in form of words and let world know about it.

When you left us, you just didn't leave a family, but you left three women in this society, who had no clue what are responsibilities, how a judgmental society would be, and most importantly on the silent struggles a woman have to fight every single day in order to raise girls! But do not worry appa, your loss has transformed us into three independent women, who fought every visible and invisible obstacles in front of us, most importantly without losing or compromising the morals that you have left us with!

Educating a girl child – might sound very cliché or even most discussed topics with thousands of pages, that we could collate for any essay and elocution competition. But trust me, it was that education and its importance that you made us believe in, had given a successful teacher, software engineer and physiotherapist to this society.

I still remember the struggles with communication in my High school, while I had the intention to quit talking with my friends in school due to inferiority I had, in communicating through English! You entered my life with role of teacher and changed it upside down! Now this book, is simply the corroboration for your perfect grooming and the impact of you within me as an English teacher. You turned all my weakness not into strength, but into one of my greatest skill and asset!

Every time when we are forced to face some ugly sides of society, and some dark shades of men, it just simply makes us to think and analyse , or even admire your qualities and the quality of life, which you chose to live , amidst of all pollution.

Not to forget, the moments of our recognition, acknowledgement, appreciations, success, reminds not about the hard path we have crossed. Just one question, arises! How appa would have reacted on this?

Appa – Will you be proud of us for achieving greater heights? Or would you be in tears of happiness? Would you be interested in social media, when we teach them to you, to repost all our success stories or our family picture in your DP? Would you be setting yardstick still high and motivate us to reach them, rather than boasting on small success?

We don't know. We really don't know. Am sure, your presence would always be missed, but I would make sure that your responsibility and duty on this family was never missed and we always fill your eyes with pride and happiness as daughters!

- From three independent woman, that you have left in this world.

Dr. Suryanka Singh

Dr. Suryanka Singh is a practicing Neuropsychiatrist and hails from Patna. She has been published in various anthologies. Her email id is suryanka2608@gmail.com.

Life Is Short...

Death, an uncharted territory...
Life was full of surprises, some beautiful, some painful...
Crossing to the other side is inevitable indeed...
Man has always chosen to suffer, to live in pain...
He has forgotten his real centre, forgotten his divinity...
Death for him means freedom from all the pain...
Death for him means freedom from all the suffering...
People believe in heaven; people believe in hell...
Death is a transition, it's a mere shedding of our bodies...
For our soul is eternal...
For I know you exist...
You exist in this vastness of nothingness...
Watching over us, rooting for us...
We miss your physical presence but there is solace in knowing that you are at peace...
Life is short... death, an uncharted territory...

Soul Is Eternal

The thoughts of death and dying scares me...
Makes me weak, gives me an uncomfortable feeling...
I don't want to imagine a world where you don't exist...
But everything comes with an expiry date...
The medicines expire, animals cross to the other side, plants wither away...
The cycle of birth and death continues...
The only relief I have is knowing the soul is eternal...
We will meet again...
Perhaps another century, perhaps as other beings...
Perhaps in another dimension, perhaps in dreams...
Perhaps on a snowy mountain in another galaxy...
Your absence kills me...
But I live, I thrive...
So long, until we meet again...

Where Have You Gone?

I wished upon a star...
I wished to see you again...
My love, where have you gone...
Vanished into thin air...
All I have is memories...
Sweet and sour memories...
I cherish every moment that I have spent with you...
You thought me to lessons of life...
We grew together, in love...
We made vows, in sickness and in health...
Till death do us apart...
My soul feels you around,
My body misses your touch, your sight, your scent, your voice...
Where have you gone...
Amidst the dark sky, I believe you shine as a star...
Watching over me, sending me your love...
I wished upon a star.. I wished to see you again…

Love

I picked you, I chose you, I loved you...
But death... Ohh the inevitable death...
My heart yearns to get a glimpse of your face...
My body misses your touch, your tickles...
My fingers miss intertwining with yours...
I feel incomplete without you...
My other half, my better half...
Where have you gone...
I hope to fall in your arms as I breathe my last...
Wait for me on the other side...
For I shall see you soon...
Our souls will merge as one again...
For our love is eternal...
Till then, I will live...
I will cherish your memories till I see you again...
I picked you, I chose you, I loved you...

Madhura R J

Presently working as a Research Assistant she believes that Life is full of opportunities, missing even one would be the reason to regret when you look back.

A passionate artist stepping into most of the field from writing, theatre, voice over, dance, anchoring to being an entrepreneur and freelancer providing services like bridal makeovers and mehendi, designing, silk thread jewellery and promoting kadhi, she is never drained of energy for the love towards her passions.

It Was Always Empty Without You

Dosing off in the chair every night,
Waking up in the bed next morning.
Walking a couple of steps,
Shifting to your arms remained the closest.
Waiting you to go deep into the nap-
Just to jump off the bed & out to play.
The constant question answer session after the nap-
You: when did you wake up?
Me: just 10 minutes before you!!
There was fear, there was respect, there was care,
Overall there was love everywhere.

Sitting in front of the television watching news.,
Debating current affairs ending to be our arguments.
From home to society, you spoke about everything
I never failed to question you until you shot
"Uff!! You should have been a lawyer"

The dresses you choose, the bangles you brought,
The streets I made you roam just for a cloth.

The regular question you had when I won group events:
'what about individual?'
Yes, I won them too but
As a child cherished the ones won with the group.
Today! I stand confident with my head held high,
Look back and see you asking the same.
You always wanted me to stand strong like today.
Of course it's the dream of every parent &
I am more than happy I could fulfil it.

We fought, we argued, you were angry I was too,

Never realized there was concern among us too.
Just because we mingled a lot,
The house seemed all tight packed.
The day you left, I realized:
'It was always empty without you'

Home is never a home without you!
I sit in the corner and think to self:
All these years I never felt how addicted I was to you.
Now loads of words still remain within,
untold and unexpressed without you.

Only a small hope:
'You are proud and happy where ever you are
as your little daughter has stood up to be the one you dreamt of'

LOVE was always there, but hidden within never expressed,
At this moment I want you to know
'I LOVE YOU AND MISS YOU THE MOST DADDY'

Riya Rashmi Dash

She is Riya Rashmi Dash presently pursuing her BBA from KIIT University, Bhubaneswar. She is Selenophile, loves to enjoy every small moment of her life, and is a wanderlust. She is a writer and started her passion 2 years back and also aspires to be future HR Manager. She has worked in more than 100 anthologies as co-author and compiler of 6 books till now and more ongoing. She is also the Author of her solo book "Waiting to Exhale"

Open Letter To My Favourite Soul Who Passed Away

Dear Neha,

It's been nearly 13 months since the day I found out I'd never see or hear from you again. A year and a half spent with you feels like 2 days when I compare it to now. July 28th was the day I realized I had to take on this crazy world without you by my side.

Death is a weird thing. One moment you could be talking & giggling, and the next you're on your knees, crying, and you can't breathe. It hits like a train, even though it takes forever to actually realize that the person who you were so close with, is gone and they're never coming back.
All I have now are memories of us. Photos, a few videos just to hear your voice, and remembrance Facebook page. That is all that's left of you… as a person. You left this Earth for God knows what reason, but he took you way too soon. No sign in sight. Nobody could have seen this coming. It's true what they say… the good die young. For what? Nobody will ever know the answer to that.

I don't think you understand just how much happiness you brought to so many people. You could light up any room you walked in and everybody knew who you were. Nobody was a stranger to you, either. You could walk up to someone and act like you knew them forever. Everyone was a friend to you.

I know you visit me and give me signs, big or little, to tell me that you're okay, but I still catch myself at the most random of times hearing your infectious laugh and voice. Maybe it's your bright smile that lights my phone up when I don't have a

notification coming through. Everyone said it gets easier, but I don't believe that in the slightest because 13 months later, I still fall to my knees and ask God, "Why her"?

Time flew. It went from minutes, to hours. Hours to days. Days to weeks. Weeks to month. Next thing I knew, it was the year anniversary. A whole year without you. In that year, the world was a pretty dim place.

I feel like I've needed my best friend more than ever and you're the reason why I need you.
From
Your best friend forever

To everyone who's lost someone too soon, know that you are not alone in your struggle in this life. Loss happens more often than you may realize, and you're surrounded by lifeguards who are ready to jump in when you need them to. There is no ocean of grief vast enough to combat the power of love. The love around you, the love in your heart and the love of the people watching over you from above — will always be strong enough to bring you back to shore.

Aishwarya Garg

Aishwarya Garg is 21-year-old dental student. She is from Roorkee city of Uttarakhand. She is an amazing writer and poet and she wants to be an influencer in future.

तुम

वो भी क्या पल थे
जब साथ हम तुम थे
खोए अपनी ही दुनिया में बाते जब होती हजार अब याद आते है वो लम्हे बार बार
तू ना है अब तो भी तेरी यादें लिए जी रहे हैं।
पन्नों को पलट तुझे याद कर देख कैसे कुछ आंसु पी रहे है।
ढलते वो दिन तारो की रात वक्त यूहीं कट जाता तेरे साथ,
जैसे वीरान पड़ी जिन्दगी मैं मेरी तू खुशी का एक नगमा था।
रंग जो भिखरा दे वो प्यारा सा एक सपना था।
तू दूर है कहीं तारों में अब छुपा पर तेरी मुस्कुराहट का रंग है यहीं ठहरा,
दिल कहीं कुछ आज उदास है जैसे मिलने को तुमसे बेकरार है।
पर अक्सर यहीं इस कोने आकर सब कह देती हूं तेरे होने को मैं यूहीं महसूस कर लेती हूं।

लोगो की भीड़ में कहीं खो सी जाती हूं अलग जब लगता है तो मैं फिर सो जाती हूं।
की कहीं सपनों में आए तू , तो मुझे देरी ना हो जाए क्योंकि दुनिया मेरी तब शुरु होती है।
याद करती हूं मैं एक फ़रियाद करती हूं तू रहें खुश जहां भीं हो मैं बस सदा यही मांग करती हूं।
हर रिश्ते का एक वक्त होता है लोग बिछड़ तो जाते है मगर उनका अक्स यहीं होता है।

हर बात हर याद हर अहसास हर वादे में जब कहीं उनकी याद आती है कुछ नमी आंखो में और लबो पे उनकी बात आती है।
एक चमक सी होठों पे आ जाती है जब कली कहीं खिल जाती है, तेरी यादें फिर यूहीं ताज़ा हो जाती है।

यह जिन्दगी की कश्ती तो यूं ही बढ़ती जाएगी कभी एक मुसाफिर तो दूसरा लाएगी।
पर दिल को छू लेना हर किसी के बस में नहीं वो अदा तो तेरे बाद भी बस तेरी ही रास आयेगी।

Ruchika Shrikant Morghade

This is Ruchika Morghade hailing from 'The City of Oranges' Nagpur. She was graduate from Shri Shivaji science college Nagpur. She Love to write in Hindi and Marathi language. She has worked as co-author in 'India Needs Change','Ansuni Aawaz' and many more and many projects in the process and many more to come.

कुछ अधुरा सा रह गया मैं...

मेरी उन छोटी छोटी उंगलियों को थामने वाला, यू मुझे अकेला छोड़ गया
जिन कंधों पे मै सोया करता था,
अब वही कंधे सो गए है
एक तेरी आवाज सुनने ,
के लिए मै आज भी तरस रहा हूं
और उसकी आस लगाकर मै, आज ज़िन्दा हूं।

पापा आप होने से मै पुरा हो जाता था,
अब आपके बिना मै अधुरा सा हो गया हूं
आप तो मेरे सासों में समाया हुआ करते थे
अब बिन सासों का कैसे जी सकता हूं मैं
मेरी हर शैतानियों को तुम सीने से लगा लेते थे
मेरी हर परेशानियों को
तुम अपना बना लेते थे
लौट आओ ना पापा,
एक बार तो, सीने से, लगा लो ना।

अब करनी है वो सारी बातें,
जो मेरे मन में खंडर सी बन गई है
अब किसे बताऊं वो सारी बातें
जो एक कमरे में कैद हो चुकी है,
उस कमरे की घुटन इतनी बढ़
गई है, की अब सांस लेने की भी जगह नहीं है।

लौट आओ ना पापा और मुझे अपने आप में समा लो ना

अब आपका नाम बड़ा करने के लिए सारी बुलंदिया भी हासिल कर ली है,पर आप के इंतजार में घायल शेर की तरफ इन राहों में भटक रहा हूं।

आज भी आसमानों में, झिलमिलतें तारे हैं, पर मेरा तारा कहीं गुम सा गया है
अब सवाल बहुत है मन में, की
मेरा तारा खो सा गया है तो,
अब मैं किस तारें का नाम रोशन करू...

पापा लौट आओ ना, और अपने घायल शेर को गले से लगा लो ना...

Siddharth Jain

He is a student and want to become a writer. He has a great passion in writing poems in every genre. He has a dream to change the poetic world for everyone.

मौत

ज़िन्दगी जीने की तो सभी सोचते हैं,
कभी मौत का ख्वाब भी नहीं देखा होगा।
एक बार मौत को जी कर देखते हैं,
जो हमारे जीवन का अटल सत्य होगा।
अरमान कई थे तो इन आखों में,
कुछ हुए पूरे और कई अधूरे रहे गए।
चार कंधे थे तो सहीं मुझे उठाने को,
पर उनसे किए कुछ वादे अधूरे रहे गए।
शाम तलक जलती चिता के लिए रोए सभी,
मन में ख्वाहिश तो थी होते उनसे रूह - ब - रूह कभी।
अंतिम मेरी यात्रा में क्या उमड़ी वो भीड़ थी,
सभी की आँखों में मेरे न होने की नमी भी थी।
मैं जिया जब तक न खुद से जीने की इजाज़त थी,
एक ऐसी ही मौत की तो फिर मेरी इबादत थी।
कैसे वो मंज़र मैं शब्दों में बयाँ कर सकता था,
मेरे पीछे हज़ारो थे, मंजिल खत्म होने पर शमशान था।
उस रात सुकून से सोया पर न जागने का ख्वाब कहाँ था,
मौत ही जीवन का अंतिम सत्य है मैं इससे अंजान कहाँ था।

Sakshi Pandey

Sakshi
Pandey

Sakshi is occupationally a student. Her works are mainly based on the emotions of different aspects of people in her society. Apart from writing she also keeps interest in painting.

Tum Chale Gaye

Vakt jaise gujar raha tha
Ab lamhe aise thahar gaye
Kal tak jo tum sath the mere
Ab jane kaha tum chale gaye

Baat na jane kya thi vo
Ki tum andar hi andar rah gaye
Keh dete ek bar mughe
Kyu khamoshi se chale gaye

Baat to thi zaroor Kuch
Jo tum akele sah gaye
Puch pati tumse kuch, uske pehle....
Tum jane kaha chale gaye

Khuddari aisi bhi kya
Ki khudgarz banke reh gaye
Bol hi dete to kya ho jaata
Jo bina bataye chale gaye

Ik pal ko tum sath the mere
Ik pal mein akela chor gaye
Khushiyon se jo jagah bhari thi
Vo khali kar ke chale gaye

Sawaloin se dukhte the jo kaan
Aaj sunne ko tumhe taras gaye
Bin bole ek kaam na karte
Aaj bina bataye chale gaye

Nikeeta Sharma

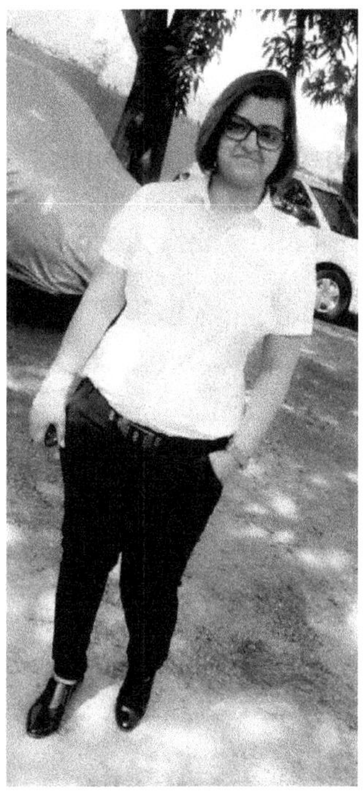

She was born to be a leader, leader of her own soul, of her own decisions, of her own life.. she believes in learning everyday from each one she meets. Running a photography company has given her thoughts wings to fly high by using creativity to its best! A hard core sports person, and a firm believer of destiny..life is her biggest nemesis but she loves to pull herself back from the downers life throws at her. An aspiring unconventional writer who loves to pen down what she feels, just as is! A humble, decent and a fighter attitude keeps her going.

Tere jaane ka ghum zindagi bhar rahega.. Tu naa aa paaya dobara toh yeh dil tanha rahega..
Iss umeed me chalengi ab yeh saansein meri
Ke aaj nahi toh kal Tu zarur lautega!!

Meri mohobbat ki daastan adhuri rahi
Tu nahi toh yeh zindagi bhi zaruri nahi..
Ek baar hi sahi, Tu waapas toh aajaa
Tere bina jeena ab mumkin bhi nahi..

Tu hai mujhme zindaa kahin
Tere hone ka magar, mere paas koi saboot nahi
Tabaahi machaa rahi hai tanhaai meri
Kaise bataaoon usse, ke Tu chuppa hai
mere hi andar Kahin..

Zindagi aur maut ko maine kareeb se dekha hai..
Khudko jalte hue aur tujhe jaate hue dekha hai..
Zindagi ko haarte hue, aur maut ko jeet te hue dekha hai..

Rooh tadpi hai agar meri tujhse Milne ko toh aatma Teri bhi tadpi hogi...
Zinda hoke bhi maut ke Kareeb hoon main toh maut Teri bhi tadpi hogi!!

Vrushali Khewale

This is Vrushali Khewale, from Nagpur, Maharashtra.
She is a teacher by profession. She has done B.A., M.A. in Sociology, M.A(MLT), B.Ed (Add), B.A. in Music and Marathi too.
She has also appeared in 'Upantay Visharad' and also cleared 'Sugam Sangeet'.
She loves to play Harmonium as well.

आयुष्य हे असच असतं

आयुष्य हे असच असतं
आठवणीच ओझ संपत नसतं
हळव अंतर खुणावत असतं
संपव जगणे हे सांगत असतं।।१।।

आठवणीचा दुजोरा घेत
काळाला म्हटले मागे जा?
काळ बोलला माझ्या सवे
आठवणीच उरल्या फक्त पाहा।।२।।

वाटेत भेटले जन,संत आणि वैरी
ओळखता न आले मज मनी
चक्रव्यूहात अडकवून आवळला त्यांनी माझा श्वास
मागे वळून बघितले, तर हाच होता सत्यभास।।३।।

आठवणी भिजल्या अश्रूंनी त्या
जाता-जाता कळले नाही मला
मरण्याआधी तू रडून घे थोडा
म्हणत होतीस तू मला।।४।।

सुखदुःखाची भरली पाने
मरण नाही तितके सोपे
दुःखाचे आभाळ कोसळले जसे
काही पाने राहीलीच कोरे।।५।।

घेतला निरोप या जगाचा
वाटलं जगायच तरी कशाला?
माझ्याच मरणाचा सोहळा बघतांना

वाटलं जगाव यांच्या करिता।।६।।

'मरण' तर सर्वांच्याच नावडीचं
स्मरणात राहत निरंतर
स्मशानच सर्वांच अस्तित्व
हेच एकदम आहे सत्य।।७।।

करुनी प्रश्न परमेश्वराला?
मृत्यूच आहे का एक सत्य?
त्यावर परमेश्वराने उत्तर दिले
पृथ्वीतलावर तुला कोणी जगू नसते दिले।।८।।

स्वर्ग आहे की नर्क आहे
ज्याचे त्याचे भाग्य आहे
हेच एकदम शाश्वत आहे
तथास्तू म्हण्यातच अर्थ आहे।।९।।

शरीर नश्वर झालं, पण गाथा नाही सरली
जगात फिरता-बोलता सत्य भटकत राही
'कर्मावर' आयुष्याच अंतिम देण अवलंबून असतं
घेईल मी पुढचा जन्म,देवालाही देण भाग असतं।।१०।।

Chirag Mehrotra

This is Chirag. He is pursuing his degree of BTech from Lucknow, He is a Social Person and a Critique Writer on Social Issues. He loves to Work actively for Society and teaching the students. He is nurturing to bring Positive Changes in the thinking of People through his writings.

आज ले ली है विदाई किसी ने अपने परिवार और जहान से
पूरी हुकूमत थी उनकी जग में जीना आता था उन्हें शान से
आज ले ली है विदाई किसी ने अपने परिवार और जहान से।
बस यादों में रह गया बसेरा बड़ी दूर हो गया घर अब तेरा
फिर नहीं होगा मेरे घर तेरा फेरा सपनों में याद आएगा
हमको बस एक तेरा चहरा बस यादों में रह गया बसेरा
बड़ी दूर हो गया घर अब तेरा। दिल का आँगन कर गये सुन्ना
तुम तो थे बरगद का पौधा हम सब तो थे इसका तना
शांति दे आत्मा को तुम्हारी प्रर्थाना करेगें उस भगवान से
आज ले ली है विदाई किसी ने अपने परिवार और जहान से।

Rancey Jain

She is Rancey Jain from Dahod.
She loves to know people. She is also part of anthologies
You can contact her on:
Instagram: Jain_Rancey
E-mail: jainrancey13@gmail.com

Dear soul

I don't know how to find you and my happiness back,
I don't know how to live with knowing people with unknown nature,
I don't know where I lost you,
I don't know where to find myself without your shadow,
I don't know how to be a good person for everyone without you,
I don't know how to cheat myself again,
I don't know where to start find you,
All I know is I want you,
without you I'm nothing,
I promise I'll be the best person who suits on your personality,
I promise I never become harsh on myself and others,
I promise I make a better house for you,
please come back because I don't know where to find you or how to live without you,
Because you are the reason of my happiest life,
Which I lost when I lost you...

Divyanshi Nayan

This is Divyanshi Nayan. She belongs to Patna, the capital of Bihar. She is a student of Std XII commerce. Apart from her acedemic achievements, she is also a poet and a co-author of more than 18 anthologies. Writing is her passion and she loves to write in both Hindi and English. It gives her relaxation and peace of mind. Her ambition in life is to become a successful entrepreneur and a writer.

She also runs a NGO named "NAYAN Mera Khwad Meri Udaan". She believes "It's time to transform ourselves, to get our destination.''

Instagram - @_beyond_ur_thoughts_22; @passionate.writer_

Dear Bapu

Today I am broken,
And my heart is in alot of pain.
For the same people are abusing you,
For whom you spent your life without a gain.

I can't explain you,
Why there is so much hate.
But it's sure those who dislike you,
Don't know that you made their fate.

Unlike them you didn't do anything,
Just for money and fame.
Still people abuse you to rise,
And that's a really big shame.

If only you returned,
And just one show your face.
Without you things are hellish,
Because we are destroying our race.

Perhaps there would be no domestic voilence,
If they read about your life.
Because all the time you taught us,
That the best man is kind to his wife.

They way you showed love to the young,
And taught us to respect the old.
If someone a tenth of you appears today,
He would have a heart made of pure gold.

You taught us we all are equal,
Regardless of our religion.

Bapu please come back!
We really need your vision.

Your Devotee,
Divyanshi

Sriya Sri

This is Sriya sri, studying bjmc 1st year from IMS Noida.Currently, she is the founder of the opus coliseum, community of publication house. she is the project head of spectrum of thoughts
She is a Hindi, english and Maithili writer belongs from Madhubani Bihar.
Just before 7 years ago she has made her debut in the world of poetry and her purpose is to take her poetry to larger stage.
She believes the saying that writing is just like Meditations.
At present she is spreading her poetry to people under the community "Speakup Mithila" .

याद

तेरा जाना इस क़दर
मेरे आँखों में चुभता हैं
तुम क्यों गये जाना
मेरा दिल ये कहता है
मेरी गुस्ताखियों को तुम
जो इतना माफ़ करते थे
तेरी यादों में अब तो दिन रात
मेरा दिल ही सेहता हैं
तम्हारी यादें भी तो
मुझसे बातें करती है
मुझसे लिपटे रहती हैं
मुझे यादों से मिलाती हैं
तुमने कहा भी था ना जब
की उम्र भर साथ निभाउंगा
क्यूँ छोड़ा बिच में साथ
जबकि कहते थे,
जन्नत साथ दिखाउंगा
तेरी बाते तभी मुझको
मेरी आंखे भींगाती थे
जो ख़ुशी के होते थे
आज गम को दिखाती हैं

Shivika Sharma

Shivika Sharma is a writer.
She is a college student.She live in kawardha Chhattisgarh. She loves to write poems,quotes & shayaris etc.She used yourquote app for presenting her views.Her insta handle is @shivika1108

ख्वाब

एक ख्वाब जिसमें तू और मैं,
एकसाथ होते थे।
एक ख्वाब जिसमें सिर्फ,
एक तेरी ही झलक दिखती थी।।

न जाने कहां खो गया वो ख्वाब,
जिसमें सिर्फ एक तेरा साथ होता था।
न जाने कहां खो गया वो ख्वाब,
जिसमें सिर्फ एक तेरा ही आस होता था।।

छोड़कर चले गया तू,
आखिर क्यों मुझे हमेशा के लिए।
आखिर क्यों मुझे इतना तड़पाया तू,
सिर्फ अपने मतलब के लिए।।

मैंने अपने दिल में,
मैंने अपने ख्वाबों में।
मैंने अपने ख्यालों में,
सिर्फ एक तेरा ही साथ चाहा था।।

लेकिन आखिर क्या हुआ तुझे,
जो इतनी जुदाई दे गया मुझे।
आखिर कहां खो गया तू,
जो इतनी तन्हाई दे गया मुझे।।

मानती हूं बिछड़ना तेरी मजबूरी होगी,
लेकिन बात नहीं करना..!
ये तो मजबूरी नहीं होगी।

यूंही किसी को अनदेखा करना,
ये तो मजबूरी नहीं होगी।।

जवाब चाहिए मुझे तेरा,
कि आखिर इतना ख्वाब दिखाकर।
क्यों दूर चले गया तू मुझसे,
आखिर क्यों दगा किया तूने मुझसे।।

और आज तू मुझे ही गलत कहता है,
छोड़कर तो तू मुझे गया है।
फिर भी मुझे गलत समझता है,
हर लम्हा मुझे सताता है।।

वो ख्वाब अब अधूरे ही रह जाएंगे,
क्योंकि जानती हूं मैं।
कि तू लौटकर वापस आएगा ही नहीं,
कि तू लौटकर वापस आएगा ही नहीं।।

Ishant Nikure

This is Ishant Nikure hailing from 'The City of Oranges' Nagpur, Maharashtra. He is a student of life science, currently pursuing graduation in B.sc (biology) from Shri Shivaji Science College, Nagpur. Project Head of Spectrum of Thoughts, an affiliate of FanatiXx. OMG book of records holder, edition 2020 for Anthology India needs a change he compiled. He has worked as a co-author in some anthologies like, Give me a break, Distance doesn't effect love and in more than 50+ anthologies. His debut anthology was "Bachpan ke Emotions"

Also a compiler of 5+ anthologies and in the process for more.

निरोप

निरोपचे दुत अवेळी
सांगावा घेऊन येणार
बघण्यास मला एकदा
तुझ्या डोळ्यातले पाणी
धावून येणार.

खचून नको जाऊ रे
मी सोबतचं राहणार,
हा! आता ओरडणार नाही तुझ्यावर
फक्त गप्प फोटोतून पाहणार.

आता तर तुझा एक
खर्च ही कमी होईल.
मेल्या म्हाताऱ्याची कट-कट
कायमची दूर होईल.

राग याईचा ना रे
तुला माझा?
जेव्हा मी बोलायचो,
तुझ्याचं पगाराचा हिशोब
जेव्हा मी तुला विचारायचो.

चुकलं रे माझं
माफ कर मला,
माझाचं मुलगा कधी मोठा झाला
कदाचित कळलंच नाही मला.

वाटलं की तू अजूनही
माझा राजा आहेस,
रोज घरी परतल्यावर

एक शब्द बोलणार आहेस.

तुझा जन्म झाला
नं ती आनंदाने रडली,
पण, मला गप्प पाहून
तुला माझी दगडी वृत्ती कळली.

तुला जरी बोलायचं
नसलं तरी,
तुझ्या फोनची वाट बघायचो
बापाचं काळीज आहे रे
तू चावला तरी धरायचो.

पण, जी चूक मी केली
ती तू नको करू!
माझ्या सारखा बाप तर
तू मुळीचं नको बनू.

तुझ्या मुलासोबत तू कधी
मोठ्याने नको बोलशील,
बापाचा तो हक्क नसतो
कदाचित तेव्हा तू समझशील.

नाहीं! अं हां अजिबात
डोळ्यातून पाणि नको काढूस
माझं पत्र उशिरा सापडलं नां रे?
फक्त शेवटचं मला घे समजून.

तुझ्या बापाला माया नाही
अशी समजूत ठेऊ नको,
काळजी घे रे पोरा
आता शेवटचा निरोप घेतो.

Eshan Gupta

Eshan Gupta is currently a 4th yr BTECH Student from Chandigarh. He is a person who loves to write, and has been writing from 2013(that's 7+yrs). He's one of those who love acting, sports (cricket, netball, football and badminton), loves to interact with people and have one unique interest that's observing people and analysing their behaviour as well.

Zindagi Ki Manzil

Kise ne kha ki uski Dua hai khuda se,
Ki kisi ko kabhi tutna na pade.
Mene kha, Yeah vo Dua hai
Jise khuda khud chate hoe bhi
Kabhi mukamal nahi kr skta.
Kyuki aksr,
Zindagi ke kise na kise mod par
Sab ko tutna padhta hai,
Kuch bikhar jate hai,
Toh kuch nikar jate hai.
Zindagi ki niyati hai badlna,
Yeah hum par hai ki tutne ke baad,
Kis raah pr mudna hai
Wo jiski mansil bikharna hai
Ya woh jiski mansil Nikhrna.
Khuda ke hath mai sab hota,
To duniya ka yeha hal na hota
khuda sirf raah dekha skata hai
Uspr chalna khud ko hi hoga.
Mera anjaam mujhe pr nirbhar hai
Mere khuda pr nhi,

Haqiqat

Khuch khash nahi hai,
Koi jadu nahi hai
Jo hai hakikaat hai
Mana duniya pyar bhi hai
Duniya mai nafrat bhi hai
Pr jo hai hakikaat hai
Mana yaha dhokhe bhi hai
Yaha sachai bhi hai
Pr jo hai hakikkat hai
Yaha muh pr kuch hai
Pithe piche kuch or hai
Pr jo hai hakikaat hai
Jubaan pr kuch hai
Or ankhoo mai kuch or hai
Jubaan pr ho hai vo hakikaat nahi hai
Pr jo ankho mai hai vo hakikaat hai
Kyuki vo hi dil mai bhi hai
Or vo hi hakikaat hai

Andhaira

Khete hai andhaire se buri or koi chiz nahi hai,
Pr, yeh andhaira hi hai, jisne mujhe yeh ehsas krvaya hai,
Ki andhere mai to khud ki parchai bhi sath chor deti hai,
Tu bure waqat mai dusro se umeed lagane ka koi matlab nahi hai

Wajib

Na tune mujhe samajhna wajib samjha
Na maine tujhe samajhna wajib samjha
Is liye shayad khushiyon ne hum dono se muh ferna wajib samjha

Rishtey

Barso lag jate hai jinko banane mai, vo rishtey khelate hai
Pal bahr se phele jo tut jate hai vi rishtey khelate hai
Dil lagane se phele jo hum bante hai vo rishtey hai
Pr jinhe aksar hum bich rah maio toddete hai vo bh rishtey hi hai
Khushi bhi yeah rishtey hi dete hai
Gam bhi yeah rishtey hi dete hai
Khuda hai ki is baat ka ehsas bhii yeah rishtey hi dilate hai
Shaitan bhi basa yaha is baat ka ehsas bhi yeah rishtey hi karate hai
Rishtey jene ki vajha bante hai
Rishtey hi hai jo marne ki vajha bhi bante hai
Rishto ko samjh pao intni aukat nhi hai
yeah sabak mujhe zindagi pal pal deti hai
Rishto ke bina zinda hokr bhi koi zinda nhi hai
yeah sabak mujhe zindagi pal pal deti hai

Yamini Sharma

She tends to find creativity in everything around her. Every story she creates, creates her, she writes to recreate herself a notch higher everytime. Being in a techie line(software engineer), she has a very unique artistic shine. She is passionate about her dreams and loves to spend time travelling, reading books. Individual who likes to spread smiles and love all around.

With the eyes closed
bad things will be opposed!
You can feel your soul
to make it whole
Whole with all the warm Love
to spread it all around the above
Above the vibes filled with negativity
to make yourself full of positivity!
You see more with your eyes closed
and the charm is imposed!
Laugh like to have the best photograph
Kiss like a bliss
Pray like a slay
Dream like to become the top cream
Is all felt with closed eyes
to see the pretty things rise!
You remember all the good
make you happy that would
in a way to feel the bliss
and your life will have a kiss
through this worries will dismiss.
That moment you will feel tranquil
and will be thankful!
Thankful for All the beautiful memories
and will leave you to your victories!

Light after the night

That shine behind the darkness
being a rise as largeness
After a black delineation
there' s always a white creation!
For those who want to see light
must have been through dark night!
Dark night exhaling hurt
makes you a little desert.
but then after all the suffer
that has been tougher
there's always a day
that makes you freeway
Freeway of all the harm
and will fill you with a little charm!
You will be much stronger
and that too for a longer
to deal with any dark stage
and that will be your happy page!
Happy page of your pretty life
that deals with ups and downs
but will make you wear crown
to go through a gleeful town!
Town that excludes the bad ones
but includes all the best ones
Ones who will be there with you always
with all the craze
just to make you feel better
plus to enjoy the battle together!
And the darkness will fade away
as soon as the arrival of a shiny day!

ज़िन्दगी..

ज़िंदगी कुछ इस तरह की
हर मोड़ पर ये सीखाती
मुँह के बल गिर कर उठना
फिर जितना भी तुम टूटना
रो रो कर फूटना
अपनी गलतीयों से सीख कर
हर वक्त आगे बढ़ना अक्सर
झेलने की ताक़त देकर
अपने आप को बनाना हमसफ़र
निकलोगे तुम इस मुश्किल दौर से
बनोगे तुम मज़बूत अंदर से
इतना अपना सब को देकर
फिर देखना एक बार खुद को लेकर
अकेले खुश पाओगे खुद को.....
दिल में नफ़रत ना रख कर किसी के लिए
सिर्फ़ और सिर्फ़ प्यार ही रखिए
आपका खुद का एक ही दिल है
जैसे भरोगे पाओगे वैसे खुद को...
प्यार कर के ना इच्छा रख प्यार की
अपने दम पर जितना हो सके हिम्मत कर उसकी
लौट कर आएगी ख़ुशी तेरे ही पास
रख फिर चाहे अपने आप को जितना भी उदास
कर बस इतना की दिल में हो प्रेम
पाओगे फिर खुद को ही अहम

Moon and the birds
Everyone will be looking at it with a different view
And that's what I already knew!
This moon seems to be in a unique style
that sums up a pretty smile
All around the sky is so white
and the moon being at a height
showing its beautiful light!
Looking at it
makes my soul split ,
Split to see the different people of world
with my nature being curled,
Curled with distinct mood swings
but giving everyone happy things!
Things filled with happiness
that will last in their life full of busyness.
And the birds flying so high
looks happy without a single cry.
This makes me feel a little low
being on the ground moving so slow
and these birds flying in a happy flow
that makes me wish I could also know
how to fly so that I could also grow!
Grow through life in an astounding way
to have my fascinating phase.
This view being a delightful clue
be my happiest crew.
Crew having chirpy hearts filled with love
and spreading it all around the above,
Above all the hatred
that should not be created!

Flairs and Glairs, a platform by a student for the students. We are esteemed youth struggling to carve out our path for our future and we follow a basic mindset Since everyone is not born with all-round skills. Joining hands with people who are born to execute it with perfection is the best way to evolve. Self-Evolution is the need of the hour but, evolving as a community is what we strive for. The initiative as kickstarted by, Founder- Mr. Shubham Shah with the motive to utilize the skillset and talent of writing has now a team of 10+ people who are actively participating into newer forms of learning and discovering talents among youngsters. We Provide platform and services like Publishing opportunities, Open mics, Workshops, Hands-on training. Operating with Brand Name of Flairs and Glairs (Publication House), we offer the chance of elevating a passionate writer to an esteemed author With Brand name Teekhe Zasbaaat. We bring to you an opportunity to get accustomed with the Public Speaking and Presenting of Thoughts along with regular challenges to brush up your inking spirit. The newest initiative to extend our services we introduced in a new writing Platform- The Glittering Fables and Ink Over Tears.

We Choose to Fly Like A Falcon than to be

a Leg Pulling Crab.

www.ingramcontent.com/pod-product-compliance
Ingram Content Group UK Ltd.
Pitfield, Milton Keynes, MK11 3LW, UK
UKHW022004190726
13853UKWH00004B/1720